STANDARD LOAN

2 8 MAR 2011

P

MCG

THE KITE AND CAITLIN

For my brother, Bob J.P.

1 3 5 7 9 10 8 6 4 2

Copyright © text Roger McGough 1996
Copyright © illustrations John Prater 1996

Roger McGough and John Prater have asserted
their rights under the Copyright, Designs and Patents Act, 1988
to be identified as the author and illustrator of this work

First published in the United Kingdom 1996
by The Bodley Head Children's Books
Random House, 20 Vauxhall Bridge Road, London SW1V 2SA

Random House Australia (Pty) Limited
20 Alfred Street, Milsons Point, Sydney, New South Wales 2061, Australia

Random House New Zealand Limited
18 Poland Road, Glenfield,
Auckland 10, New Zealand

Random House South Africa (Pty) Limited
PO Box 337, Bergvlei 2012, South Africa

Random House UK Limited Reg. No. 954009

A CIP record for this book is available from the British Library

ISBN 0 370 32371 8

Printed in China

THE KITE
AND CAITLIN

Roger McGough

Illustrated by John Prater

The Bodley Head
London

The kite hadn't been out of the cupboard since the day it had arrived at Beech House.

On her fifth birthday, Octavia had unwrapped the parcel excitedly, pulled a face, and then passed on to the next gift.

And there were many.

Kites are not cuddly.
You cannot dress and
undress a kite.
You cannot wear one.

Kites do not miaow.
You can't curl up in
front of the fire
with a good kite.

The kite spent its first day behind the sofa, and the next fifteen years in the cupboard under the stairs.

Caitlin's mother came across it at a car-boot sale. "Just the thing for Jack," she thought.
But Jack thought differently.

You can't play football with a kite.
You can't strum one.
You can't shoot aliens with
a kite.

A kite cannot be
plugged into the television.
A kite does not make an
unbearably loud noise.

The kite might have spent the next fifteen years in another cupboard
had it not been for Caitlin.
What Caitlin loved about the kite was its sadness.
She understood it.
The last two years had been spent in and out of hospital.
She was weak and could not walk.

"When you get better," said her mother, "you will be able to go up on a hill and fly the kite."

Mother and daughter smiled at each other. A sad smile. One that stayed in place too long to be true.

"I want to fly it from the top of a mountain," said Caitlin.

"A mountain, indeed," said her mother, "and which one did you have in mind?"

"I don't know yet," said Caitlin, stroking the kite's tail, "but one day I will."

Soon, Caitlin knew all there was to know about mountains (or rather, knew a little of all there was to know about mountains).

She learned that the highest mountain in Britain is Ben Nevis (1,342 metres).

That the highest mountain in Europe is Mont Blanc (4,807 metres).

That the highest mountain in Africa is Kilimanjaro (5,895 metres).

That the highest mountain in the U.S.A. is Mount McKinley (6,194 metres).

And that the highest mountain in the world is Mount Everest (8,848 metres).

8,848 metres

6,194 metres

5,895 metres

4,807 metres

1,342 metres

But more than the cold facts she liked the cold photographs. Against a blue sky, the mountain-tops standing head and shoulders above people, pain and important things. In touch with infinity, tête à tête with the stars, sharing the secrets of the universe. Mighty summits where the winds were strong enough to breathe life into kites and keep them aloft for ever.

It is Midsummer's Eve. So hot that nothing moves. In the garden, the leaves hang limp on the trees. The lawn wrinkles its brow trying hard to remember rain.

Only the cat is cool, curled up in a pool of moonlight.

In her bedroom, Caitlin lies on the bed limp as a leaf. Each breath a shadow of the one before, every heartbeat a fading echo.

High summer, and a leaf is about to fall from the tree.

"Hold tight," whispers the kite.

"Hold tight, and I will take you where the air is so fresh and pure, one breath is all you need."

And out of the window
and up into the windless sky
and over the parched fields
and the dry tongue of the river
and the cracked lips of the hills ....

"We're going to a mountain,
aren't we?" asks Caitlin.
But the kite is silent now.

And up
and over
Loch Ness
(the monster
fast asleep in
the ice-box
of the deep).

"Is it Ben Nevis?"
asks Caitlin.

And up
and over
the Welsh Valleys
(the sheep on the
hillsides counting
each other before
dozing off).

"Is it Snowdon?"
asks Caitlin.

And up
and over the
Channel and
across France
(the Alps slumbering
beneath a satin sheet).

"Is it Mont Blanc?"
asks Caitlin.

And up and
over the Adriatic
into Greece (the
gods moonbathing
and longing for
bygone days).

"Is it Mount Olympus?"
asks Caitlin.

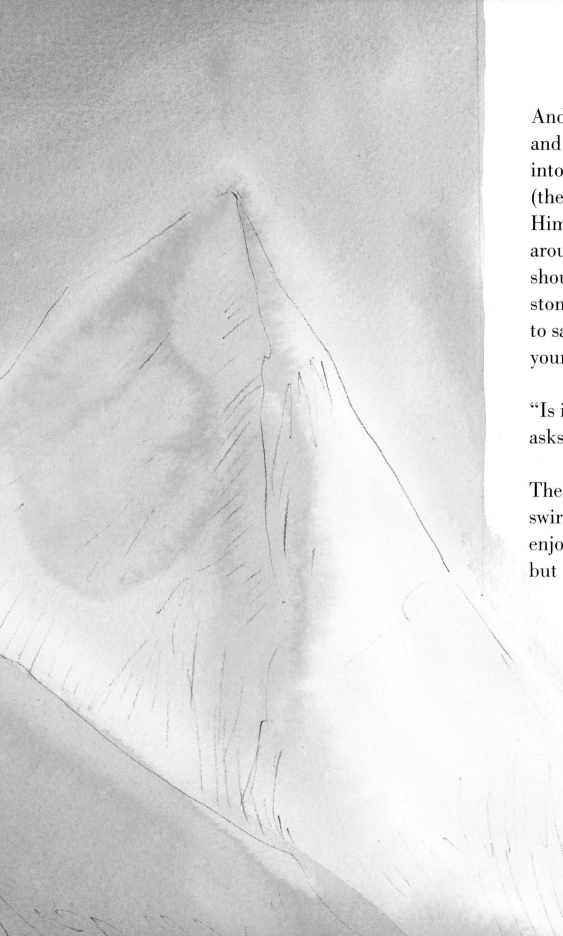

And up
and over India
into Nepal
(the giants of the
Himalayas, arms
around each other's
shoulders, glaring
stony-faced as if
to say: "Visit us at
your peril.")

"Is it Mount Everest?"
asks Caitlin.

The kite stoops and
swirls around the top,
enjoying the moment,
but doesn't stop.

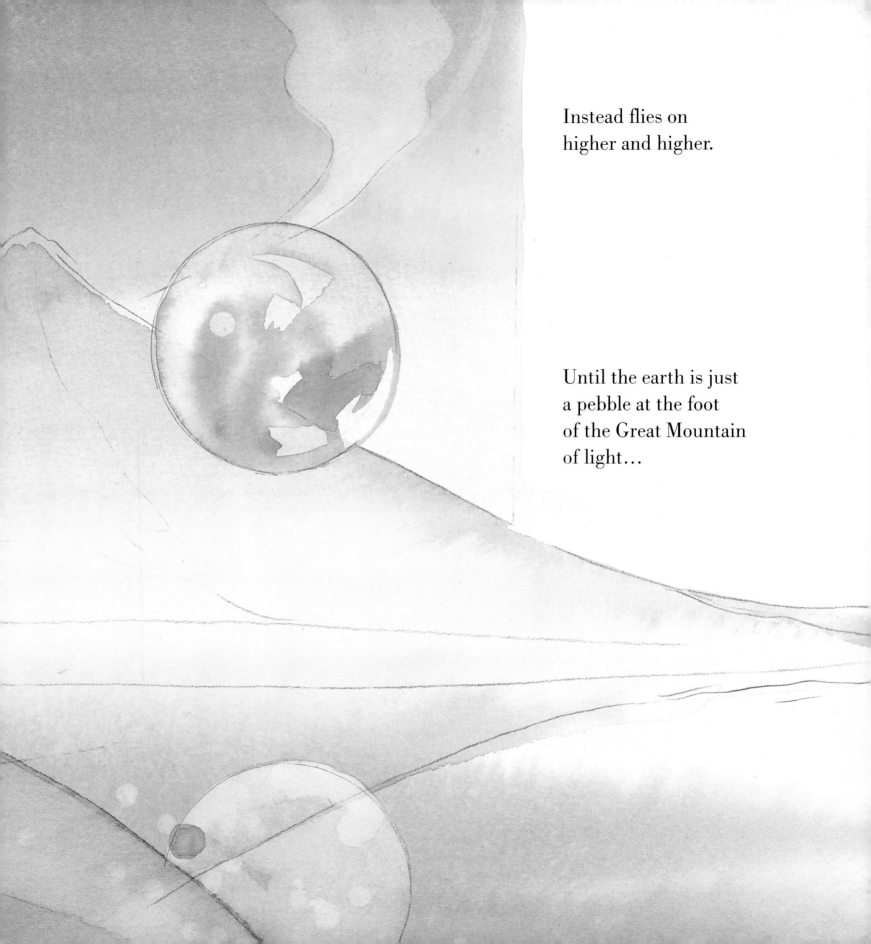

Instead flies on
higher and higher.

Until the earth is just
a pebble at the foot
of the Great Mountain
of light…

…where happiness ever after waits for
Caitlin and the kite.